MW01155966

Lerner **SPORTS**

SPORTS ALL-STARS

CHRISTIAN PULISIC

Jon M. Fishman

Lerner Publications ◆ Minneapolis

SCORE BIG with sports fans, reluctant readers, and report writers!

Lerner Sports is a database of high-interest biographies profiling notable sports superstars. Packed with fascinating facts, these bios explore the backgrounds, career-defining moments, and everyday lives of popular athletes. Lerner Sports is perfect for young readers developing research skills or looking for exciting sports content.

LERNER SPORTS FEATURES:
- ☑ Keyword search
- ☑ Topic navigation menus
- ☑ Fast facts
- ☑ Related bio suggestions to encourage more reading
- ☑ Admin view of reader statistics
- ☑ Fresh content updated regularly

and more!

Visit LernerSports.com **for a free trial!**

Lerner SPORTS

Copyright © 2022 by Lerner Publishing Group, Inc.

All rights reserved. International copyright secured. No part of this book may be reproduced, stored in a retrieval system, or transmitted in any form or by any means—electronic, mechanical, photocopying, recording, or otherwise—without the prior written permission of Lerner Publishing Group, Inc., except for the inclusion of brief quotations in an acknowledged review.

Lerner Publications Company
An imprint of Lerner Publishing Group, Inc.
241 First Avenue North
Minneapolis, MN 55401 USA

For reading levels and more information, look up this title at www.lernerbooks.com.

Main body text set in Albany Std. Typeface provided by Agfa.

Library of Congress Cataloging-in-Publication Data

Names: Fishman, Jon M., author.
Title: Christian Pulisic / Jon M. Fishman.
Description: Minneapolis, MN : Lerner Publications, 2022 | Series: Sports all-stars (Lerner sports) | Includes bibliographical references and index. | Audience: Ages 7–11 | Audience: Grades 4–6 | Summary: "Christian Pulisic burst onto the soccer scene when he was still a teenager, launching him to play pro for England's Chelsea Football Club. Learn about his career, training, and what he does outside the sport"— Provided by publisher.
Identifiers: LCCN 2021002193 (print) | LCCN 2021002194 (ebook) | ISBN 9781728420554 (library binding) | ISBN 9781728423111 (paperback) | ISBN 9781728420578 (ebook)
Subjects: LCSH: Pulisic, Christian, 1988—-Juvenile literature. | Soccer players—United States—Biography—Juvenile literature. | Soccer midfielders—United States—Biography—Juvenile literature.
Classification: LCC GV942.7.P84 F57 2022 (print) | LCC GV942.7.P84 (ebook) | DDC 796.334092 [B]—dc23

LC record available at https://lccn.loc.gov/2021002193
LC ebook record available at https://lccn.loc.gov/2021002194

Manufactured in the United States of America
1-49150-49298-3/29/2021

TABLE OF CONTENTS

LEFT FOOT,
RIGHT FOOT, HEAD

Christian Pulisic (left) celebrates his first hat trick with Chelsea FC.

Chelsea Football Club (FC) had won three games in a row when they faced Burnley FC on October 26, 2019. One big reason for Chelsea's success was forward Christian Pulisic.

FACTS
AT A GLANCE

- **Date of birth:** September 18, 1998

- **Position:** forward

- **League:** Premier League, United States Men's National Team (USMNT)

- **Professional highlights:** played his first pro game at 17; transferred to Chelsea in 2019; became the youngest player to score a hat trick in Chelsea history

- **Personal highlights:** spent most of his childhood in Hershey, Pennsylvania; played soccer, basketball, and golf as a kid; loves to eat at Chipotle restaurants

Pulisic runs with the ball in the October 26, 2019, game against Burnley FC.

In his first season with the team, he was becoming the most exciting player on the field.

With the score 0–0, Pulisic streaked between three Burnley players. He took the ball and sprinted toward the goal. A Burnley defender tried to cut him off, but Pulisic dodged and kept running. He blasted a shot with his left foot. The ball rolled past three defenders and the goalkeeper and into the net.

Pulisic got the ball again just before halftime. He ran down the center of the field with three other Chelsea players. He could have passed the ball to an open teammate. But Pulisic felt confident. He banged a right-footed shot to give Chelsea a 2–0 lead.

In the second half, Chelsea's Mason Mount took a corner kick. The ball soared toward Pulisic, and he was ready. When it reached him, he smashed a header into the net. Pulisic's third goal gave Chelsea a 3–0 lead. He had scored with his left foot, his right foot, and his head for the hat trick. At 21, he became the youngest player to score a hat trick in Chelsea history.

Chelsea beat Burnley 4–2. As a new player, Pulisic began most games on Chelsea's bench. But against Burnley, he proved he was ready for a much bigger role.

"PRETTY GOOD"

Christian playing for Germany's Borussia Dortmund in 2016

Christian Pulisic was born in Hershey, Pennsylvania, on September 18, 1998. He has an older brother, Chase, and an older sister, Dee Dee.

The town of Hershey is known for Hersheypark, a chocolate-themed amusement park.

Their parents, Kelley and Mark Pulisic, had played soccer at George Mason University. After college, their father played pro indoor soccer for the Harrisburg Heat.

When Christian was four, he joined a youth soccer league near Hershey. His parents coached his team. Christian liked playing, but he wasn't focused during games. "He would look at people on the sidelines and wave at them as the game went on around him," his father said.

In 2005, his mother accepted a teaching job near Oxford, England. Seven-year-old Christian moved to England with his family. Playing for the youth team Brackley Town, Christian's interest in soccer took off. He said, "I just started to love it so much and I said: 'Wow. I'm pretty good!'"

After a year in England, Christian and his family moved to Michigan. His father coached the Detroit Ignition, a pro indoor team. Christian played for the Michigan Rush youth team.

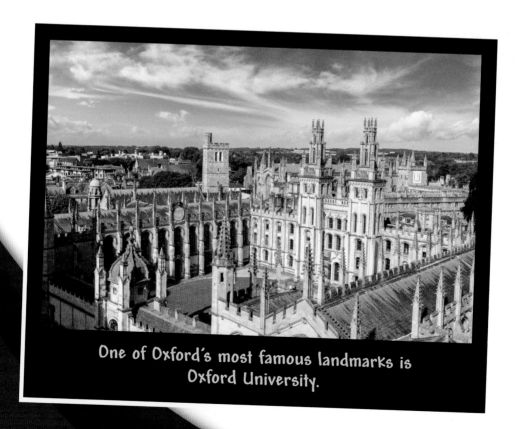

One of Oxford's most famous landmarks is Oxford University.

Youth soccer players can play for development academy teams to improve their skills.

In 2008, the family moved back to Pennsylvania. Christian began playing in the PA Classics league. The league is part of the U.S. Soccer Development Academy. The academy trained young US athletes to play at soccer's highest levels.

Christian stood out on his PA Classics teams. His speed impressed his coaches. He was a strong passer and shooter with both feet. During games, he made lightning-quick decisions.

Christian's skills caught the attention of coaches with the US Men's National Team (USMNT). In 2012, he began playing for USMNT youth teams. Over the next two years, he scored 21 goals in 28 games against other youth national teams.

Germany's Bundesliga is one of the top pro leagues in the world. In 2015, Christian agreed to play for the league's Borussia Dortmund. That July, he moved to Germany with his father. Christian trained with the team and played his first league game in January 2016.

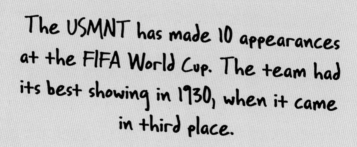

The USMNT has made 10 appearances at the FIFA World Cup. The team had its best showing in 1930, when it came in third place.

Christian steals the ball in the April 2016 game against Hamburger.

Christian made history in an April game against Hamburger. He stole the ball from a Hamburger player and blasted it into the net. The goal made him the fourth-youngest scorer in Bundesliga history. He also became the youngest player not born in Germany to score in the league. Christian had proven he could succeed against the world's top players.

SHARPENING HIS SKILLS

Christian playing for the US Men's National Team in 2016

Christian started practicing soccer as soon as he could kick the ball. He watched his father's games and copied the players' moves. At home, he watched soccer games on TV.

During practice, Christian works to improve his speed and quickness.

During halftime, he would run out to his yard to practice the plays he'd just seen. Then he'd rush back inside to watch the second half.

Christian didn't just try out the moves he saw—he mastered them. He practiced moves again and again until they felt natural. He also made sure he could do them well with both feet.

To avoid feeling burned out with soccer, Christian picked up other activities too. He played basketball, golf, and other sports. Playing several sports helped Christian to learn new skills and build his confidence.

With PA Classics, Christian learned to play all around the soccer field. His coaches didn't force him to stay in certain areas. They gave him the freedom to work on his skills and choose his own position. Given Christian's speed and scoring ability, the forward position was a natural fit.

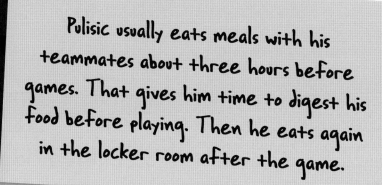

Pulisic usually eats meals with his teammates about three hours before games. That gives him time to digest his food before playing. Then he eats again in the locker room after the game.

Pulisic stretches before a training session. Athletes often stretch to warm up their muscles before a workout.

Before joining Borussia Dortmund, Christian didn't spend much time using exercise equipment. Instead, he used his own body weight to get stronger. He did exercises such as push-ups and pull-ups, lifting his body to strengthen his muscles.

After moving to Germany, he began using weight-lifting equipment. But pro teams often play three or four times each week. That doesn't leave a lot of time for workouts. Christian usually hits the gym twice each week. But he gets plenty of exercise zooming around the soccer field.

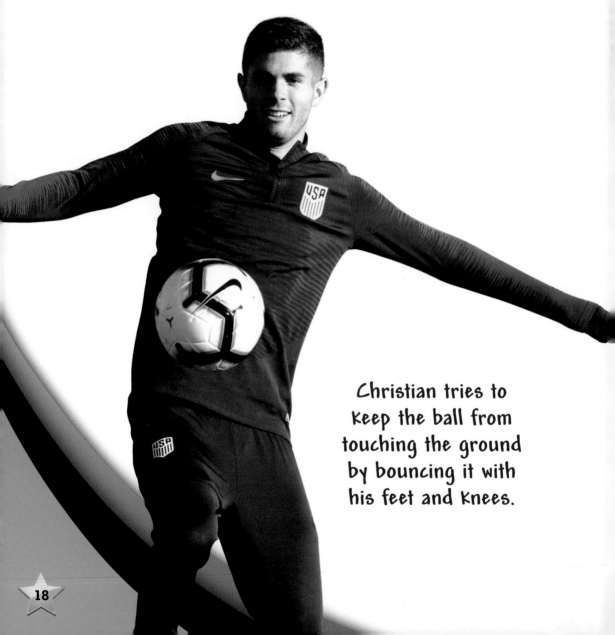

Christian tries to keep the ball from touching the ground by bouncing it with his feet and knees.

TEENAGE SUPERSTAR

Pulisic runs with the ball in a February 2019 game.

In Germany, no sport is more popular than soccer. During Borussia Dortmund home games, fans wearing yellow jerseys fill the stadium. Together, they form the Yellow Wall.

The Yellow Wall never sits down. Fans cheer, chant, and sing to inspire their team to win. They quickly embraced Pulisic. When he came onto the field, 80,000 Dortmund fans shouted as one: "Pulisic!"

At first, all of the attention made Pulisic nervous. But as he scored goals and thrilled fans with his moves, he began to relax and have fun. Pulisic quickly became a celebrity in Germany. People often recognized him on the street.

Dortmund fans stand during the whole game to form the Yellow Wall.

Christian signs a ball for a fan in 2018.

Borussia Dortmund paid Pulisic more than $8 million a year. At 17, he had become a rich and famous athlete. But in some ways, he was still just a normal teenager. In May 2016, Pulisic practiced with the USMNT in Kansas City, Missouri. At the end of the month, he took a break from practicing to travel to Hershey for his high school prom.

After the prom, Pulisic flew on a private jet back to Kansas City. On May 28, the USMNT faced Bolivia's national team. With the US ahead 3–0, Pulisic received the ball in front of Bolivia's net. He fired a low shot to score. The goal made Pulisic the youngest player to ever score for the USMNT.

Pulisic after he scored for the USMNT against Bolivia in May 2016

Burrito Fan

One of Pulisic's favorite places to eat is Chipotle. After games, he often has a chicken burrito from the restaurant. In January 2020, Pulisic became Chipotle's first international ambassador. He helps to promote the restaurant in the United States and Europe.

In April 2020, Pulisic teamed up with Chipotle to help hospitals. A new disease, COVID-19, was spreading around the world. Pulisic and Chipotle organized free weekly meals for overworked doctors and nurses who were treating people with the disease.

Chipotle is a restaurant chain that serves burritos, tacos, and other food.

CHELSEA AND BEYOND

Pulisic played his last home game for Dortmund in May 2019.

Pulisic played four seasons with Borussia Dortmund. He scored 13 goals in 90 games with the team. On January 2, 2019, Dortmund transferred him to Chelsea in

England's Premier League. Chelsea paid Dortmund more than $73 million for Pulisic. The deal made him the most expensive US player in soccer history.

Pulisic was thrilled to play in the Premier League. "This was a big dream of mine and I feel this was the right time to make this step," he said.

Pulisic in his first game with Chelsea FC

Pulisic played his first game with his new team on August 11, 2019. Chelsea lost to Manchester United 4–0. But on October 26, he scored his first goal for Chelsea. He scored twice more in the game to complete the hat trick and lead Chelsea to victory.

Chelsea has won the Premier League five times. They won their last league championship in 2017.

Pulisic chases the ball in December 2020.

Chelsea had a winning record in 2019–2020, but they finished fourth in the Premier League. Pulisic scored nine goals in just 25 games. He has a bright future in soccer, and his numbers are sure to keep rising. He plans to lead Chelsea to their next Premier League championship.

Player	Goals	Minutes played
Tammy Abraham	15	2,215
Christian Pulisic	9	1,722
Willian	9	2,600
Olivier Giroud	8	993
Mason Mount	7	2,867
Jorginho	4	2,379
Marcos Alonso	4	1,430
N'Golo Kanté	3	1,732
César Azpilicueta	2	3,229
Antonio Rüdiger	2	1,710

Glossary

ambassador: a person who represents a company or government

Bundesliga: the top pro soccer league in Germany

corner kick: a direct free kick taken from the corner area after the ball is played out of bounds past the goal line by the defending team

forward: a player who plays near the opponent's goal

hat trick: three goals in a single game by a player

header: a shot or pass made by hitting the ball with the head

Premier League: the top soccer league in England

pro: short for professional, taking part in an activity to make money

prom: a formal dance given by a high school or college

promote: to help a product to grow and develop

Source Notes

9 George Dohrmann, "The Christian Pulisic Blueprint," Bleacher Report, June 7, 2017, https://bleacherreport.com/articles /2713937-the-christian-pulisic-blueprint.

10 "Christian Pulisic: 10 Things You Might Not Know about Borussia Dortmund's USA Star," Bundesliga, accessed December 1, 2020, https://www.bundesliga.com/en/news /Bundesliga/christian-pulisic-10-things-on-borussia-dortmund -s-nascent-usa-star-459300.jsp.

20 Sharyn Alfonsi, "Will Christian Pulisic Be the Next Big Name in Soccer?," CBS News, last updated January 2, 2019, https:// www.cbsnews.com/news/60-minutes-will-christian-pulisic-be -the-next-big-name-in-soccer/.

25 Andrew Keh, "For Christian Pulisic and Dortmund, Chelsea Transfer Was a Team Effort," *New York Times*, January 9, 2019, https://www.nytimes.com/2019/01/09/sports/christian -pulisic-dortmund-chelsea.html.

Learn More

Chelsea Football Club
https://www.chelseafc.com/en

Greder, Andy. *Behind the Scenes Soccer*. Minneapolis: Lerner Publications, 2020.

Premier League
https://www.premierleague.com/home

U.S. Men's National Team
https://www.ussoccer.com/teams/usmnt

Williams, Heather DiLorenzo. *Chelsea FC*. New York: AV2 by Weigl, 2020.

Young-Brown, Fiona. *Chelsea FC*. New York: Cavendish Square, 2020.

Index

Photo Acknowledgments

Image credits: AP Photo/Simon Bellis/CSM via ZUMA Wire, pp. 4, 5, 6; AP Photo/ Guido Kirchner/picture-alliance/dpa, p. 8; © Rj1020 via Wikimedia Commons, p. 9; S-F/Shutterstock.com, p. 10; Gregory Rec/Portland Press Herald/Getty Images, p. 11; AP Photo/Guido Kirchner/picture-alliance/dpa, p. 13; AP Photo/Carlos Herrera/ Icon Sportswire, p. 14; AP Photo/Adam Davy/PA Wire, p. 15; AP Photo/Matt Dunham, pp. 17, 18; AP Photo/Press Association, p. 19; AP Photo/Martin Meissner, pp. 20, 24; AP Photo/Mark Von Holden, p. 21; AP Photo/Colin E. Braley, p. 22; Ken Wolter/Alamy Stock Photo, p. 23; REUTERS/Alamy Stock Photo, p. 25; AP Photo/David Klein/CSM, p. 27.

Cover image: Action Foto Sport/Alamy Stock Photo.